Naughty
STORIES for
Good boys and girls
CHRISTOPHER·MILNE

*The Toilet Rat of Terror*
*and Other Naughty Stories for Good Boys and Girls*
published in 2011 by
Hardie Grant Egmont
Ground Floor, Building 1, 658 Church Street
Richmond, Victoria 3121, Australia
www.hardiegrantegmont.com.au

A CiP record for this title is available from the National Library of Australia

Text copyright © 2011 Christopher Milne
Illustration and design copyright © 2011 Hardie Grant Egmont

Illustration and design by Simon Swingler
Typesetting by Ektavo
Printed in Australia by Griffin Press, an Accredited ISO AS/NZS 14001:2004
Environmental Management System printer.

The paper this book is printed on is certified by the Programme
for the Endorsement of Forest Certification scheme. Griffin
Press holds PEFC chain of custody SGS – PEFC/COC-0594.
PEFC promotes environmentally responsible, socially beneficial
and economically viable management of the world's forests.

PEFC/21-31-26

1 3 5 7 9 10 8 6 4 2

**Other books by Christopher Milne**
The Day Our Teacher Went Mad and Other Naughty Stories
The Bravest Kid I've Ever Known and Other Naughty Stories
The Girl Who Blew Up Her Brother and Other Naughty Stories
An Upside-Down Boy and Other Naughty Stories
That Dirty Dog and Other Naughty Stories
The Girl With Death Breath and Other Naughty Stories
The Crazy Dentist and Other Naughty Stories

**Also available from www.christophermilne.com.au**
The Western Sydney Kid
Little Johnnie and the Naughty Boat People

the **toilet** rat of terror

GRRR

**- AND OTHER -**

# Naughty
# STORIES FOR
# Good boys and girls

CHRISTOPHER MILNE

Illustrations by
Simon Swingler

hardie grant EGMONT

# TO PETE AND ROB

Peter and Robert are my two sons and they
provided the inspiration for most of my stories.
They have always been a bit naughty in
real life, but also brave, clever, decent
and funny – and much-loved.

Pete and Rob went to Nayook Primary School
and many of these stories are loosely
based on those wonderful years.

*Christopher McCabe*

# contents

# the toilet rat of terror

Damien Kelly had heard the rumours. He'd even heard some of the screams. But it didn't worry him.

'Giant rats biting people on the bottom!' said Damien to anyone who would listen, shaking his head. 'Some kids will believe

anything. It's time they stopped acting like cry-babies and got a life.'

Unfortunately, it was a rumour he should have listened to. Damien fancied himself as the toughest, no-nonsense kid in school, and believing scary stories was for wussies. But people who try to act tough are often big cowards underneath, and it's usually just a matter of time before it all comes crashing down. Damien was about to find out what a nasty fall it could be.

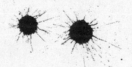

It all began with Joseph Jabour, another kid from school. He was sitting on the toilet at

home, minding his own business, when he heard a really strange noise. A low, swishing noise. Although he couldn't explain it, he started to get a weird feeling that something bad was about to happen.

Grrrrrrrrr!

Joseph jumped! Was that a growling sound he had just heard?

*I know,* thought Joseph, starting to sweat. *It's probably just that stray cat trying to steal Thumper's bone.*

## GRRRRRRR!

*Of course,* thought Joseph, grinning nervously to himself. *The baked beans I had for lunch.*

But if Joseph had looked down, he wouldn't have grinned for much longer. Crouching beneath him, in the middle of the toilet bowl, was a rat the size of a dog! A dripping wet rat with greasy fur, narrow eyes and teeth bared – dirty, yellow teeth smeared with blood and filth and disease.

Its eyes were fixed on poor Joseph's bare bottom and you could tell from the shivering muscles in its legs that it was only seconds away from pouncing.

Three, two, one...

'ARGH!'

The bite was so big and painful that Joseph shot forward onto the bathroom floor with

the door left swinging behind him. He had a huge chunk missing from his bottom and his head was spinning. What could possibly have happened? Some sort of terrible trick played by his brother?

Later, as the doctor gave him a tetanus injection and stitched up the massive bite, he said that his tests showed Joseph had been bitten by a rat.

'A rat?' said Joseph's mum. 'How could that be? Our house is always spotless.'

'Could it have come up through the bowl?' asked Joseph, trembling. 'Through the pipes?'

'I don't think so,' said the doctor. 'Unless there's a rat that's able to hold its breath

under water, it has to have jumped in.'

'But I would have seen it,' said Joseph. 'I always check the bowl first for floaters.'

'Too much information,' said the doctor.

Joseph's mum had gone quiet, deep in thought. 'Unless…' she said.

'Unless what?' asked the doctor.

'My husband works for the government making radio-active isotopes for medical research,' said Joseph's mum. 'I don't have to tell you how dangerous they can be.'

'Like what Homer Simpson does,' chipped in Joseph.

'This mustn't go any further,' added Joseph's mum, 'but he told me there have

7

been leaks over the years that might have found their way into drains. And there were rumours of something weird near one of the drain openings – a sort of mutant rat but with scales and fins like a fish. And it's supposed to be huge!'

The three of them just stood there staring at each other. Surely it couldn't be true?

'Right,' said the doctor. 'You must keep this totally to yourselves until we can prove it. People have a right to know, but not until we're sure. Panic is the last thing we need. Don't want people getting all nervous and running to the toilet, do we?'

The doctor's little joke fell flat.

Of course, Joseph did say something at school. How could you not? The rumours began. And then more stories of bites and screams. One girl said the rat that bit her had wolf-sized jaws. Most people said they heard a swishing sound of a rat coming up through the pipes and then that same terrible growling sound that Joseph had heard.

Finally, Damien Kelly decided it was time to act. He reckoned he'd never heard such a load of rubbish in his life! What a bunch of nervous nellies. Believing in fish-rats! It was time to prove how wrong everyone was.

'I know all the drains around here like the back of my hand,' said Damien. 'Been up every

one of them a thousand times. So, I'm going in and I'm going to show you pack of sooky babies that there are no giant rats coming up through the dunny! And guess who's coming with me to see that I'm right? The baby who started it all in the first place. Joseph!'

Joseph felt sick. Not the drains! They were creepy and scary and his parents had told him a million times how dangerous they were. There were holes and drops at every turn, and he'd even heard about kids who went in and never came out. But how could you say no to Damien?

You should have seen the crowd around the entrance to the drain as they went in.

Probably a hundred kids had turned up. Joseph was white with fear, but Damien was loving it. He'd worn his army-type camouflage pants, a black T-shirt and big steel-capped boots. He had a torch and, just in case, a huge cricket bat.

Damien had been waiting all his life for a moment like this. To be the fearless hero in front of a huge crowd. And he'd also been waiting to say these words – just like army guys on TV...

'I'm going in!' yelled Damien, as the kids all cheered.

The first bit of drain was sort of OK, because Joseph could still look back to see

the entrance, and plenty of light shone in. But then it got really dark and, although Damien's torch lit the way ahead, the drain walls turned to black. Joseph thought he heard something and he jumped.

'What was that?' asked Joseph, shaking.

'Probably a rat,' replied Damien, tapping the cricket bat against the drain wall a few times. 'There's thousands of them down here. Seen a few snakes, too.'

Further and further they went in. It felt to Joseph as though they must have travelled at least a couple of kilometres. That sick feeling was getting really strong, and he thought he might faint.

'Looks like I was wrong,' said Joseph weakly. 'There's nothing here, is there?'

'Oh, there's something here all right,' said Damien. 'You can't see them but there are rats all around us. Look!'

Damien swung his torch up and there, sitting on a concrete shelf, were a hundred pairs of gleaming eyes. Joseph felt himself go wobbly at the knees. And then they heard it. That low, growling sound.

Damien froze. 'Is that the noise you reckon you heard?'

Joseph's mouth was dry with fear. 'Ye-es.'

'Don't move,' whispered Damien, suddenly sounding a bit strange. 'There is

something and it's close.'

He slowly ran the torch light along the walls, and what they saw next took their breath away. Poking out from a huge hole in the wall was a giant rat's tail. With scales!

All Damien's toughness left him in a flash. Without realising it, he grabbed hold of Joseph's arm in fear. 'Can you see that?' he asked, trembling.

Damien really had believed that they'd find nothing. Now that he'd seen this terrible half-fish, half-rat monster, he felt himself turning to jelly.

Damien's shaking meant the torch was

bouncing about, but not enough for them to miss seeing the tail move. The giant fish-rat was starting to crawl towards them.

The boys stood there, frozen with fear. The creature's body was covered with stinking, greasy fur and patches of sharp, nasty-looking scales. Slowly, the fish-rat began to lower itself into a pouncing position. Its lip curled back to reveal foul blood-stained teeth and the growling began again.

We all do things differently when something scary comes along. Some of us run, some of us freeze and some of us choose to fight. Joseph would definitely have put fighting the rat last on his list, but to his great

surprise, he suddenly found himself getting braver. One of them had to do something, or they'd both be attacked!

The growling was getting louder, so Joseph knew he only had seconds to act before the rat pounced. He reached over to take the cricket bat from Damien's limp hand, and just as he did, the fish-rat jumped. Straight at him like a dog in a terrible fight. Joseph grabbed the bat and swung it wildly!

As the giant fish-rat flew straight at Joseph's throat, the cricket bat whooshed through the air, straight at the fish-rat's open, snarling mouth.

In cricket terms it would have been a six

over the grandstand but, when you added the speed of the fish-rat, its impact with the cricket bat was explosive. Like a watermelon being hit by a speeding truck. Teeth and scales and face and guts went everywhere. Some of it even flew into Damien's open mouth.

With one almighty whack, Joseph had killed the thing stone-dead!

'That'll teach you to bite me on the bum,' he said.

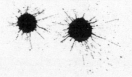

Well, the fish-rat problem went away after that, and Joseph and Damien became heroes.

'Why Damien as well?' you might ask.

Well, Joseph's such a nice bloke he said they had killed the fish-rat together. The two of them are mates now, and Joseph opens the batting for the school cricket team.

There is one small problem, though. The huge amount of water people are using to flush their toilets — sometimes six or seven times at a go. It's the centimetre-thick steel mesh everyone has screwed in at the bottom of the bowl — just in case.

# the girl who was left behind

Kathy Crawford hated Christmas. Sure, she liked the presents and stuff from her foster family, but Christmas reminded her most of what she didn't have. A real mum and dad.

Well, that's not quite true. Kathy did still have a mum. Somewhere. But her mum

didn't want to see her anymore.

That might sound terrible, but sometimes mums and dads feel it's better for someone else to look after their kids, even though they love them very much. The new mum and dad are called 'foster parents'.

Usually it happens because the real mum and dad are poor. Or because they can't find somewhere to live. Whatever it is, it had always got something to do with awful sadness.

Sometimes, the real parents will visit their kids, or even have them home for weekends. Other times, however, the mums and dads feel so guilty about what they've

done, they don't even ring. And so it was with Kathy's mum. Poor Kathy, she hadn't heard a word for six years. Not since the day she was left sitting on a seat at West Park Shopping Centre.

On that terrible day, Kathy's mum put her in the lovely coat she'd bought from the op-shop and then took her shopping. Kathy knew something was wrong because her mum kept crying all the time. More than usual. And why would they be going shopping? Sure, it was only a week before Christmas, but Kathy knew they didn't have any money!

Her dad, who Kathy had never even met, was supposed to send some money every

week, but he never did. Kathy's mum got some from the government, but by the time she'd paid the rent and bought food, there was never much left.

So, Kathy and her mum caught a bus that day to West Park Shopping Centre and just hung around for a while. They looked in the shop windows but they never went in. All the time Kathy's mum held her hand really tight.

'What's wrong, Mummy?' asked Kathy.

'Nothing, darling,' said her mum. But Kathy knew there was.

Her mum blew her nose, took a deep breath, looked around and sat Kathy down on a seat outside the toy shop.

'Listen to me,' said her mum. 'I want you to wait here while I go to the supermarket. Don't move, OK?'

'Yes, Mummy,' said Kathy.

'Kathy, I want you to be a very good girl. Always,' said her mum. 'And remember that I love you very, very, very much. And one day…'

But that was as far as she got, because she started crying again. She squeezed Kathy's hand once more, turned, and was gone.

So, Kathy waited. And waited. *What could Mum be doing?* she wondered. *She's been gone for ages.*

Finally, a policeman came up to her and

said, 'Kathy Crawford?'

'Yes,' said Kathy.

'Sweetheart,' said the policeman, 'we've had a phone call from your mum and she's asked us to look after you for a little while.'

So far, 'a little while' had been six long years.

Kathy went to a special house for kids without mums and dads. The people were very nice and explained to Kathy that her mum still loved her, but she had to sort her life out a bit. Her mum was sick and needed time to get better.

In the pocket of the coat she had worn on that last day, Kathy found a locket with a picture of her mum inside. Poor Kathy, day after day, night after night, she just stared at the picture and wished she was back with her mum.

Kathy had only been in the house for a month when it was time to move in with her foster family. Her foster mum and dad were very nice people, but they could never replace her real mum.

For a while, Kathy was a good little girl, just as her mum had asked. But soon she became naughty. You see, Kathy was getting tired of waiting for her mum to get

better. Maybe she'd never get well. And why didn't she ring? Had Kathy been tricked?

Maybe her mum didn't love her after all. Poor Kathy, it made her angry. And nasty.

Her foster brother and sister were lots of fun, but that didn't stop Kathy from being terrible to them. She set fire to her foster brother's cubby house and stuck her foster sister's dolls down the toilet. She played frisbee with her foster dad's CDs and broke her foster mum's best dinner set with an axe. One day, on a Sunday drive, Kathy deliberately threw up in the back seat. All over the picnic basket.

Her foster family never got angry with

her, though. They just said they loved her very much and understood exactly how she felt.

When people are nice to you for long enough, it makes you nice too. Kathy stopped being so naughty. But she never forgot her mum. Until Kathy found her again, there would always be something missing.

Finally, Kathy couldn't stand it. She just had to find out the truth. Did her mum just stop loving her? Was her mum OK? Was she still alive?

So, one Saturday morning, about a week before Christmas, Kathy started looking. She knew her foster parents couldn't tell her

anything – they weren't allowed to – so it was up to her. Where she would go or who she would ask, she wasn't quite sure, but she had to try.

Kathy put her mum's locket in her pocket, picked up the old coat she had worn that day, told her foster mum she was going to a friend's house, and walked out the door.

In the beginning, poor Kathy had no luck at all. She had looked in the phone book, but couldn't find a thing. Then she walked around and around trying to find something, anything, that would lead her back to their old house. But without knowing the address, it was impossible. All she could really remember

was a broken window and a white door with a funny old knob.

And then she saw something that gave her an idea.

In the street, straight ahead of her, was a crowd of people gathered around a caravan. Inside the caravan was a man speaking into a microphone. It was one of those things where radio stations do a show from somewhere special – usually to advertise the opening of something. This time it was a new supermarket.

Kathy walked over and watched for a while. She noticed that every time the man spoke, he pushed a button. And when he

played a song, he pushed another button.

*Right,* thought Kathy, *I know this is very, very naughty, but I'm going to do it.*

Kathy sneaked around the back of the caravan and quietly opened the door. Then, just as the man had a sip of coffee while a song was playing, Kathy jumped inside and bumped the man so he spilled hot coffee all over his lap.

She pushed the button and grabbed the microphone. 'Mummy!' she yelled. 'It's me. Kathy. Kathy Crawford. Remember? Mummy, if you're there somewhere, I still love you…'

Before Kathy could say any more, the man

switched the button back and grabbed her wrist. So she bit his hand and ran as fast as she'd ever run in her life. Down a side street and then another street to a crowded park. To safety.

What would she do now? If her mum did happen to hear her on the radio, there was no use waiting near the caravan because the police would be waiting for her. And then her mum might arrive and Kathy wouldn't be there!

Poor Kathy cried. What to do now? Maybe she should go back to where it all started. Back to West Park Shopping Centre. Maybe the people in the toy shop would remember

something. Maybe her mum would do the same thing. Maybe not. Maybe her mum didn't ever want to see her again.

Kathy caught a bus to West Park and sat on a seat at the bus stop. For a very long time she just stared into space. Thinking. She felt cold and lonely and scared. Scared to go back to that toy shop and all the terrible memories that went with it.

Finally, she worked up the courage. West Park had changed a lot but the toy shop was still there. So was the seat outside, but she could hardly bring herself to look at it. She ran past and into the shop.

Kathy walked straight up to the shop lady

33

and said, 'This is going to sound so stupid, but I lost my mother outside here six years ago. Can you help me?'

The lady looked very surprised. 'Now that's amazing,' she said. 'There was a lady in here just five minutes ago asking almost exactly the same thing.'

Kathy didn't wait to hear any more. She rushed outside and there, sitting on the seat, was a lady. The lady turned and looked at Kathy.

'Mummy!' screamed Kathy.

'Kathy!' yelled her mum.

They raced to each other and her mum threw her arms around Kathy and hugged her

very, very tight. She was crying and said not a day had gone by without her feeling sick about leaving. She said she hadn't stopped loving her for a single minute, and could Kathy ever, ever forgive her. And Kathy's mum kept holding her tight for a very long time. As if she would never let go again.

And she didn't.

# the girl who wrote rude poems

Jane Stoltz stood in front of her whole class and read out the following poem:

> Some are small and some are large
>
> And it's true that we've all got 'em.
>
> But my favourite teacher, Marj,
>
> Has got the biggest bottom.

'How dare you!' screeched Mrs Marjorie Jolley. 'Stand in the corner. You may be clever with words, young lady, but nothing excuses rudeness. I've told you before and I won't tell you again!'

Trouble was, that's almost exactly what poor Mrs Jolley had said the last time. And the time before that. I guess I'd better explain.

Our principal, Mrs Staley, had decided that Jane Stoltz was a genius. A star poet in the making! Sure, she'd won a couple of prizes and stuff – in fact, the All Schools Prize for Poetry – but I didn't think she was that good.

Mrs Staley was so proud, especially

because she got to accept the All Schools Prize on Jane's behalf. She said Jane should be an example to us all. Which meant that Jane got away with much more than she should.

'I'm sorry!' Jane had pleaded to Mrs Jolley. 'Let me try again. This time, not rude.'

'Promise?' asked Mrs Jolley.

'Promise,' said Jane. 'How about this?'

'Some are big and some are huge,
But it's safe to bet,'

Then Jane paused, as if searching for words.

'Until you see my teacher's butt,
You ain't seen nothing yet.'

'That's it!' screamed Mrs Jolley.

'Go to the principal's office.'

Jane marched up to Mrs Staley's office and for the umpteenth time was given a good talking to.

'You have such a great talent, Jane,' said Mrs Staley. 'It breaks my heart. Why waste it on silly poems about bottoms? Why not do more poems like the one you won a prize for — about nature and trees and butterflies?'

'Because I'm bored,' said Jane. 'I want to do real poems. About people. Exactly like they are. The good and the bad.'

'Which is exactly what a good poet should do,' said Mrs Staley. 'But there comes a time, young lady, when we have to get serious.'

And Jane noticed that, suddenly, Mrs Staley was very serious indeed. 'The All Australia Schools Competition is exactly three weeks away today,' she said, with a gleam in her eye, 'and I'm expecting your very best poem about nature. Do I make myself clear? I'm not just **hoping** you'll win, I'm **expecting** that you'll win with your **very best poem.** Lose, and I wouldn't want to be in your shoes!'

'Hey, that rhymes,' said Jane. 'Lose, shoes…'

But Mrs Staley wasn't smiling.

Well, this is what Jane read at the All Australia Schools Competition:

# Nature

As autumn leaves fall to the ground,
and pods and seeds and nuts,
I squash a snail that I have found
and see its brains and guts.

For nature is a wondrous thing,
a beauty to behold,
the newborn lambs, the birds that sing,
and maggots, so I'm told.

For maggots do the marvellous job
of eating up dead meat.
Though sadly, and I hate to dob,
they smell like my dad's feet.

So though most nature can be great
and we are very lucky,
at times it's less than pretty, mate,
More pooey, foul and yucky.

Jane didn't win the All Australia Competition. Or any other for that matter. She decided that competitions weren't worth the worry. And Mrs Staley became such a pain that Jane decided to swap to another school. It was nearer to her home, anyway.

Jane quickly made friends at her new school and she ended up doing very well. And later went on to university. These days she works in advertising and publishes her own poems.

When Jane first started at her new school, however, her teacher said she'd heard about her poetry prizes and asked if Jane would make up a new poem to read to the class.

The teacher didn't ask ever again, though,
because this is what Jane wrote:

Disgusting acts, I'd seen a few

And thought that none could beat it.

The Edwards sisters, Jan and Prue,

Would pick their nose then eat it.

Until the Mortons, Anne and Ted,

Who picked and ate non-stop.

'Those Edwards girls are weak,'
they said.

'You watch,' they yelled, 'we swap!'

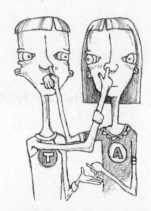

# nightood! ghost

Simone Morris thought she must be losing it. Three mornings in a row her mum had yelled at her for leaving her clothes on the floor — yet all three nights before, she was sure she'd folded them neatly and placed them on the chair.

'So what happened?' asked her mother. 'Did a ghost come in during the night and tip them off?'

'Please don't say that!' said Simone quickly.

'Where is this ghost thing coming from?' asked her mum. 'That's the third time this week! Let me say it again. There are no such things as ghosts!'

'Yes, Mum,' said Simone, now absolutely sure there **must** be ghosts. Her clothes had been pushed onto the floor three times. What else could it be?

The whole ghost thing had started with a girl from school, Rebel. Although everyone said Rebel was a bit mad, because she was

kind of weird and her parents were hippy types, Simone thought she was all right.

'Where do you think we go when we die?' Rebel had said one day. 'All the stuff in your head — all the memories and stuff, do you think it just disappears into thin air?'

'I've never really thought about it,' replied Simone.

'Well, it's time you did,' said Rebel. 'It's like light. You can't grab hold and it doesn't weigh anything but if you shine a torch out into space the light goes on forever. Ghosts are just people going on forever.'

That had really spooked Simone. She felt a cold shiver down her back and suddenly

the whole world seemed a bit scarier. From that day on, she refused to think about ghosts. Otherwise she knew she'd be too scared to sleep at night without the light on. And so far, so good. That is, until her mother had made that stupid joke about a ghost moving her clothes!

That night, frightened out of her wits, Simone lay in bed with her eyes wide open, the light on and her softball bat under the blanket. She couldn't tell her mum and dad she was scared because they didn't believe in ghosts. She'd just have to tough it out herself by not falling asleep.

Two o'clock in the morning went by,

then three o'clock, and still her clothes lay folded up on the chair. Three-thirty, the eight o'clock alarm…

Wait, what? Eight o'clock! She had gone to sleep after all. Oh, no! Lying on the floor were all her clothes, just like the mornings before. But this time they were in a circle!

Now Simone knew for certain that there was a ghost. And the ghost knew that she knew!

When Simone walked into the kitchen for breakfast, she was white with fear. Her mum took one look at her and asked if she was sick. The silly thing is, although her mum would probably have let her stay at home, Simone

thought she'd rather go to school. Anything other than staying in her bedroom with a ghost!

'I'm fine, Mum,' said Simone. 'Didn't sleep too well. Must have eaten too much last night.'

'That ghost didn't come to get you, did it?' said her mum, trying to make another joke. 'They say that children are ghosts' favourite things. Kids and animals.'

Simone shuddered and went even whiter.

If poor Simone thought it was impossible to become any more scared, she only had to wait until the next morning. Because she was so tired from the night before, she had again

fallen asleep. But this time she was awoken by her mother shouting.

'Simone, you've gone too far!' yelled her mother. 'Making a joke of my poor father. You're disgusting!'

Simone had no idea what her mother was talking about. Until she sat up and saw her clothes on the floor. This time, rather than forming a circle, they were arranged neatly to spell 'Alan'. The name of her grandfather, who had died the year before!

Simone felt sick with worry. After her grandfather had died, Simone and her family had shifted into his house. It was bigger than theirs and it had a huge backyard.

Simone went straight to her brother Richard. 'When Grandpa died,' Simone asked, trembling, 'do you know which room he was in?'

'Your room, I think,' said Richard.

That was it! There was no way Simone was going to spend another night in that room and she didn't care what her parents said.

Of course, her mother said there was no way that Simone would be sleeping anywhere else and it was time she stopped playing these stupid games. As punishment for the terrible joke she had played, Simone could go straight to her room every night after dinner for the next two weeks. And no

television or computer!

Simone started to get angry. Really angry. *I haven't done anything wrong, and I'm getting punished for it!* Once she started getting angry, a strange thing happened. She stopped being scared.

She thought, *If I don't care anymore about the stupid ghost, then why don't I just wait up and ask what its problem is?*

So, that night, Simone waited up, absolutely determined not to go to sleep. She even turned out the lights so that the ghost would turn up like usual.

But when she heard a noise at her window, all her courage seemed to leave her. The fear

came flooding back and she just sat there, wide-eyed, as a flash of light seemed to dart across the room. It couldn't be! Standing next to her window was a young girl completely covered in lace. A ghost!

Slowly, the lace seemed to peel away, and the girl moved silently to Simone's chair and began placing all her clothes on the floor. Simone's fear was so great she couldn't move. Gradually, however, a feeling began seeping into her bones that, although the ghost was only metres from her bed, it wasn't going to hurt her.

The ghost's movements were gentle and quiet and not really scary at all. Simone

couldn't believe it. Here she was in the room with a ghost and yet she was starting to feel comfortable, almost as if she knew her!

And then it hit her. Simone did know her!

'Rebel!' yelled Simone. 'What are you doing in my room?'

Rebel got such a fright she dropped to her knees. 'You frightened me half to death!' she said.

'Hello?' replied Simone. 'You're in my room playing ghost-girl and you're telling me you're scared?'

'I am so sorry,' said Rebel. 'I've been coming in through your window for days and

I thought you were a heavy sleeper.'

'**What?**' asked Simone, more shocked than angry.

Rebel began to cry. 'Because I'm so lonely,' she sobbed. 'I know everyone thinks I'm mad, and I haven't got a single friend in the whole world. You're the only person who even speaks to me at school. I just thought if I could make you believe in ghosts, then you might think I was right about them. That I'm not a complete nutter… Simone, I am so sorry.'

Simone wanted to stay angry, especially because of how much trouble she was in with her mum, but when she saw the terrible

sadness in Rebel's eyes she couldn't help but feel sorry for her.

Well, Simone and Rebel are good friends these days, but there's something I should tell you. Simone's mum was right. There are no such things as ghosts. But there are plenty of people who will tell you they've seen one. I'd be more scared of them if I were you.

# Dreamy Drake

'Dreamy' Drake Johnson was one of those really annoying kids who thought he was better than everyone else.

If you spoke to Drake, most times he wouldn't even bother to listen. If he did, he'd get bored and drift off halfway through.

'Earth to Drake?' you'd say. 'Testing.'

But no response.

I suppose it came from his snobby parents, who loved themselves so much they thought their first born child must surely be the most talented and intelligent little darling to have ever attended our school.

I even heard Drake say one day that the only reason his parents sent him to mix with us losers at Warren Flat Primary School was so he'd appreciate a 'good' school later on.

Not only were Drake's oldies rich and snobby, they were strange, too. They fancied themselves as being a bit alternative and creative and clever. They were into

brown rice and hairy legs and things dangling everywhere – 'witchy stuff', my mum called it.

For some reason, they also thought carpet snakes were cool. So there were always a couple slithering about the house. Once, when I went to Drake's house to get a shared lift for a school excursion, I was met by this dirty great thing curled around a curtain rod.

Drake wasn't quite as keen on snakes as his parents, so he slept out the back, in a specially designed carbon-friendly eco-tent. With his pet rats. Ugly-looking things they were, too. One looked as if its head had been through a blender.

How he could live with such disgusting-looking things amazed me, because the one thing we did know about Drake was that he had a weak stomach. When he saw me pick up a dropped sandwich from the ground, brush it on my shirt and eat it, he spewed everywhere.

Anyway, when Drake wasn't being a total snob, he spent the rest of the time in a dream. Most times he would have a dopey grin on his face, because he was either thinking about how wonderful he was, or imagining himself at his 'good' school when he could at last mix with some PLH — People Like Him.

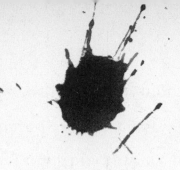

Even though Drake thought he was so much better than us, we still didn't understand why he wanted to stay in his own little dream world all the time. Wouldn't it get lonely? And what was so bad about us all, anyway?

But no-one could ever get through to him to ask. In the end, I just stopped trying.

I suppose he thought we just weren't worth talking to. He did his schoolwork well enough – in fact, he was really smart – but try getting him to play bockers with us, or footy, or chuck stones, or swap lunches, or muck

around down at the drain or do anything normal? No way.

And so the days and then years went by with Drake in his dream world and, from Drake's point of view, us in our loser world. My dad said that was the way Drake's father thought, too. He'd overheard him one day call the rest of us a waste of space.

My father said it was Drake's dad who was the idiot. 'Doesn't he know head-bands went out twenty years ago?'

By Year Six, though, something very strange happened. Drake started to speak. And listen.

You know how I said before that he was

smart? Well, suddenly we couldn't shut him up, because Drake had become desperate to prove just how smart he was.

Answering this question, answering that one, showing over and over again what a pack of meat-heads the rest of us were.

Guess why? To impress Candice Wyman. My girlfriend! Drake had suddenly discovered girls, and of all the girls in the school, he had to pick mine!

Well, sort of mine. I'd never really spoken to her but my best friend, Snotty Smith, had told Candice's best friend that I liked her and that was all you had to do. I think.

It was really good because when you

wanted to dump someone, you could do it the same way.

Well, one day we'd had this test and Drake said to me, so everyone could hear, 'By my calculations, I did better than you by thirty-two percent.'

'Yeah?' I said. 'By my calculations, you're a jerk. A jerk in trouble because you're going to get decked.'

Guess who got decked instead? Drake beat me easily. He had me down on the ground in a head-lock in about two seconds.

How embarrassing! I was the first guy ever to get decked by Drake. Out of the corner of my eye, I could see Candice whispering,

'What a loser.' I don't think I've ever felt so bad.

What could I do to get back at him? Drake was stronger than me. And smarter. Maybe I could set traps for his pet rats? Or sneak a carpet snake into his bed?

And then I thought of it. The perfect way to get him back.

The next day was a school trip to the snow. I knew that we'd be going by bus and I knew Drake would be sitting next to Candice. Pretending not to care where I sat, I just happened to flop down right behind them.

Then, as soon as we left, I took one of my little brother's books out of my bag and

67

pretended to read. 'I can't understand most of this,' I whispered loudly to myself. 'What does this word mean?'

Of course, Drake heard me – which is exactly what I wanted. Being such a smarty pants these days, Drake couldn't resist saying, 'Would you like me to read to you, little boy?'

'Well, yes I would,' I replied. 'Mum and Dad said I've got to improve my reading, so they've given me something hard.'

'Oh,' said Drake, taking the book. 'Poor little boy. Now, let me see. Oh, yes, I can see what you mean. It is a bit hard for you.'

And so Drake began to read out loud,

of course making sure that everyone was listening. 'John had a ball. John bounced the ball. John and his sister, Betty, had a dog called Spot.'

Of course, all the other kids laughed their heads off, so Drake kept going. 'Am I going too fast for you?' he asked. 'They also had a cat called Fluffy. Spot and Fluffy.'

And then it happened. Suddenly, Drake went quiet. He started to look a bit green.

You see, Drake had been reading in a bus that was going along some windy roads.

Drake was feeling sick. **Very** sick.

Straight away, I leant over and whispered in Drake's ear:

'Yellow maggot custard,

Dead dog's lick,

All washed down with
A cup of cold sick!'

Well, I've seen some barfs before, but this one would have to have been a world record. Drake spewed all over himself, all over the seat and all over Candice. Isn't it funny how there's always a bit of carrot?

It's also funny how Candice doesn't even talk to Drake these days. In fact, she's back with me. I've even spoken to her, too. By my calculations, that puts me in front by exactly **thirty-two percent** — wouldn't you agree?

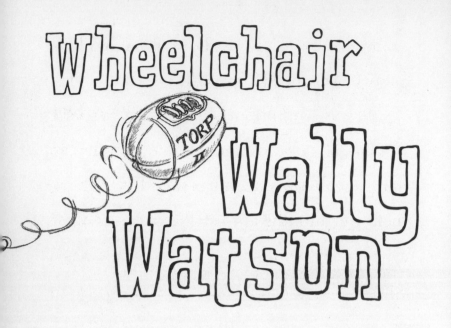

# Wheelchair Wally Watson

Wally Watson was the most fantastic kid I'd ever known. He was great at football and cricket, brilliant at video games, popular with girls, tough if he had to be and easily the smartest kid in class. But never a suck. He could reach the ceiling in the boys' toilets,

do monos for as long as he wanted and kick a footy over the library roof.

He was awesome at music, too. **Blurter music.** You know how some people can make a really good trumpet sound by pressing their wet mouths against the backs of their arms and blowing really hard? Wally was a natural. For a laugh during class, he could even do really wet, stinky-sounding blurters.

He'd also worked out that he could change the sound by blowing or pressing in different ways, and he got so good that he learnt how to blurt the national anthem. He offered to do it into the microphone at school assembly, but our principal said no.

As I say, you couldn't meet a better kid than Wally.

**That is, until the accident.**

A whole gang of us were hooning around at the local pool – bombing girls, running when we shouldn't on the wet concrete, flicking each other's bums with towels – when someone yelled, 'Hey, watch this!'

There was no problem getting us to watch, because flying through the air was a bare bottom. It was Wally, doing a reverse somersault with full moonie.

**SPLASH!**

We all laughed so much that no-one noticed Wally was taking a long time to

come up. **Too long**.

Wally had hit his head on the bottom of the pool. And broken his neck.

Wally Watson would spend the rest of his life in a wheelchair.

Wally was a mess after the accident. I've never seen anyone so sad. The fact that he could never run again, or hoon around at the pool, or play cricket… it seemed to him like the end of the world.

Eventually Wally started back at school. He did his work well enough, but gone was the spirit, the sense of fun, the cheek. That was when I spoke to him. For the first time as just the two of us, really. You see, although I knew Wally, I was never one of his best mates. Not because he didn't like me – it was just that he was so good at everything, and I wasn't. I was never part of the main gang.

You know how at school there's always a special bunch of good guys that everyone wants to be like? Well, I was on the outside, looking in.

The day I talked to Wally, we were going up to the top of a hill that overlooked the sports oval, to watch the school cross-country finals. Wally would've been in one of the races

for sure, before the you-know-what.

The hill was pretty steep and Wally seemed to be having trouble wheeling himself to the top. So I asked if he wanted me to give him a push.

'What do you think I am?' snapped Wally. 'A cripple?'

'Well,' I replied, 'maybe you could give me a push. I'm stuffed.' And with that, I sat on his lap.

Wally wasn't quite sure what to do. But he didn't get a chance to decide, because suddenly we were rolling down the hill at a million kilometres an hour. Then across the oval and down another hill and straight

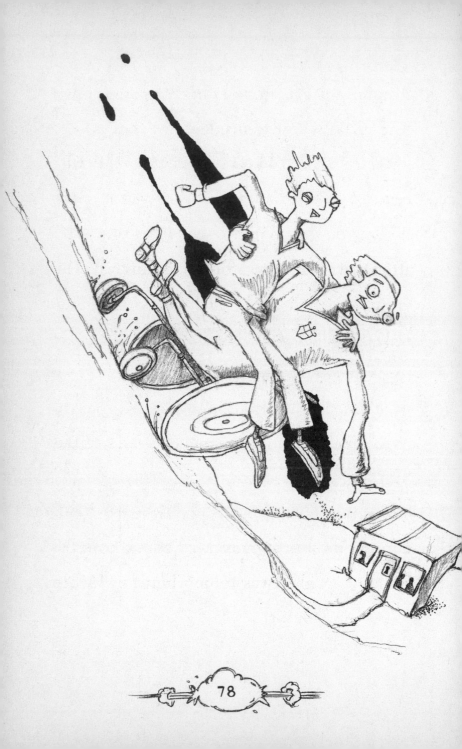

through a door into the girls' change rooms! And guess who was inside?

**Girls! Lots of them.** Without a single thing on.

Do you think Wally and I weren't popular after that? With the other boys, anyway. The questions came so fast my head was spinning. **Wally and I loved it.** We told some terrible lies, too.

After that, Wally and I became the best of friends. Wally said I'd shown him that at least some of the time, life could still be fun.

One day, for a brief moment, I thought I might've even given him some hope of walking again. I was telling him how Mum

and Dad only let me watch my rubbish TV if I saw some good things as well. They'd made me watch a show about how scientists can grow new skin and give injections of stuff to fix nerves and maybe spinal chords and…

'Stem cells,' interrupted Wally. 'Already done it. And look at me.'

'But they said it would take time to work,' I said hopefully.

'Got plenty of that,' replied Wally, with a sad smile.

Wally still did a lot of sad smiling. Although he had his good times, he had some terrible ones as well. Sometimes, I'd see him crying so hard I thought he would never stop.

When Wally had his bad times, he'd sometimes ask me to wheel him to the top of a hill overlooking our town. We lived in the country and the whole town wasn't that big, so you had a great view.

It was a grassy, lonely sort of hill, and always windy. But from there, Wally could see everything that reminded him of the good times. The football ground where he won a game with a kick on the siren. The swimming pool where summer seemed to go on forever. The old shed where he'd made a secret fort. And the exact spot where Charlotte Reed helped him to his feet and softly held his hand after he fell out of the tree.

Wally and I would talk for hours about the old days, re-living things over and over again. And then one day, something came to me. I said, 'Wally, if we can remember things and get excited all over again, even more excited than we were at the time…then maybe we could use our minds to get excited about things that we haven't done yet. Like, if you could imagine running or playing footy again, maybe it could be just as much fun. You've lost your legs, Wally, but you haven't lost your head.'

But Wally didn't say anything. He just looked at me.

'And don't forget the stem-cells treatment

you had,' I said. 'You said it didn't work, but maybe in your head you haven't given it a fair go.'

And then it happened.

**Wally's foot moved.**

'Wally, your foot! I gasped.

But still, Wally just kept looking at me. And then a smile spread across his face.

I can't explain what happened next. Wally gripped the arms of his wheelchair and slowly stood up. He took his hands away, wobbled a bit, found his balance, and took one very small step forward. Then another step, and another, and then started jogging. Then he ran – slowly at first, then flat out –

down the hill, with the wind in his face, screaming, 'Yes!'

Did Wally **really** get up and run that day? Or was it just in our imaginations?

I say he ran.

# Perfect for reading anywhere!
## Collect them all today.

Write your shopping list on a piece of dunny paper!

www.christophermilne.com.au

# ABOUT THE AUTHOR

When successful actor and screenwriter
**Christopher Milne** became a father, he found
himself reading books at bedtime to his two boys,
Peter and Robert. He soon ran out of stories
to read, so he started making up his own.

He quickly discovered that if he told Pete and Rob
about good boys and girls doing very good things
all the time, they were bored stupid.

But if he told them about naughty kids doing **pooey,
rotten, disgusting** things, his sons would scream for
more. 'We want more of those naughty stories!'

'OK,' Chris would reply. 'But only if you've been good.'
And so the **Naughty Stories for Good Boys and Girls**
were born...

For more info on Christopher Milne and his books, go to
## www.ChristopherMilne.com.au